STICKER STORIES

Sticker Fun for Everyone!

Celebrate America!

Illustrated by Eric Sturdevant

Grosset & Dunlap
An Imprint of Penguin Group (USA), Inc.

Text copyright © 2010 by Penguin Group (USA) Inc. Illustrations copyright © 2010 by Eric Sturdevant. All rights reserved.
Published by Grosset & Dunlap, a division of Penguin Young Readers Group, 345 Hudson Street, New York, New York 10014.
GROSSET & DUNLAP is a trademark of Penguin Group (USA) Inc. Manufactured in China.

ISBN 978-0-448-45392-7   10 9 8 7 6 5 4 3 2

It's the middle of summer—what a great day!
The annual parade is coming our way.

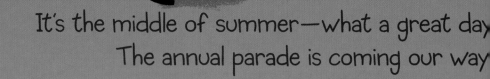

Use the stickers to decorate the scene

We're off to the park for the three-legged race.
We get a big prize if we come in first place!

Use the stickers to decorate the scene.

We cool ourselves off with a swim in the lake.
We scream and we laugh at the splashes we make.

Use the stickers to decorate the scene.

6

The food on the barbeque sure does smell great!
We gather around and pile food on our plate.

Use the stickers to decorate the scene.

Then we spread out a blanket under some trees.
We pick someplace shady that has a nice breeze.

Use the stickers to decorate the scene.

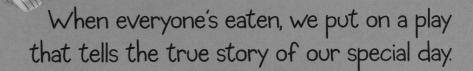

When everyone's eaten, we put on a play
that tells the true story of our special day.

Use the stickers to decorate the scene.

As the sun starts to set, the band plays its song,
and soon everybody is singing along.

Use the stickers to decorate the scene.

The fireworks burst in the sky up above,
as we all celebrate this country we love.

Use the stickers to decorate the scene.

Use these stickers
on pages 2-3

Use these stickers
on pages 4-5

Use these stickers
on pages 6–7

Use these stickers
on pages 8–9

Use these stickers
on pages 10–11

Use these stickers
on pages 12–13

AMERICA

CELEBRATE!

Use these stickers on pages 14-15

Use these stickers on page 16